How do I PUBLISH my book?

Sarah Houldcroft

Published by Goldcrest Books International Ltd
www.goldcrestbooks.com
publish@goldcrestbooks.com
ISBN: 978-1-911505-92-1
eISBN: 978-1-911505-93-8

"Books are the treasured wealth of the world and the fit inheritance of generations and nations. Books, the oldest and the best, stand naturally and rightfully on the shelves of every cottage. They have no cause of their own to plead, but while they enlighten and sustain the reader his common sense will not refuse them. Their authors are a natural and irresistible aristocracy in every society, and, more than kings or emperors, exert an influence on mankind."

Henry David Thoreau,
American author of *Walden*

CONTENTS

*"There is no greater agony than bearing
an untold story inside you."*

Maya Angelou

INTRODUCTION

Wherever you are in your writing journey, *How do I PUBLISH my book?* will prevent your words from languishing on your laptop gathering dust for months or even years simply because you didn't know what to do next.

I am the founder of the publishing company, Goldcrest Books, and have been working closely with authors for the past 10 years. Over that period, I have helped a great variety of authors writing on a wide range of subjects to both write and publish their books. Some business owners I help have no idea how to share their specialist knowledge and begin their book; some fiction writers have a head full of wonderful characters waiting to jump onto the page. All my clients' books are different, but the one thing my author clients all have in common is they always had questions about the publishing process, whether that was where to find an agent, how to copyright their work or what to do once they had finished writing.

Over the years, I have been asked many questions about publishing and have given advice on a huge number of related topics. I have done this through my coaching courses, workshops and speaking events or just over the phone to put my client's mind at rest. But the question I still get asked more than any other is simply *how do I publish my book?*

This book is short and to the point and will answer the specific question *how do I publish my book?* With the knowledge you gain from reading this book you will have a much better idea how to proceed and fulfil your dream of becoming a published author.

If you have already written a first draft, *How do I PUBLISH my book?* will help you work through all the steps you need to take in order to make your book ready for your readers. On the other hand, if you are just dipping your toe into the idea of writing your book, it will give you an overview of what to expect once you have your idea and start writing. This book will help you plan ahead and get organised regardless of what stage you are at.

As you work through this book you may wish to add your own notes. So I have included a couple of pages at the back for this purpose.

My aim in writing this book was not just to answer the question 'how do I publish my book?' but also to inspire you to dust off those manuscripts and documents on your computer, laptop or phone. You may have worked hard to get to the point where you are thinking about how to publish your book. So I want to make it as easy as possible for you to get to the next stage so you can ultimately reach your dream of becoming a published author.

WHAT ARE THE OPTIONS FOR PUBLISHING?

The publishing industry has changed such a lot over the past few years, and as I write this in the spring of 2020 there are now several types of publishing available to the fiction or non-fiction writer. As the industry seems to be continually evolving in the light of all the changes in the world and within the UK itself, this may well change again in the coming years. In the past, we have seen traditional publishing dominate the industry and then the emergence of vanity publishing which meant that individual authors were able to publish a book without going through a publishing house. However, these new authors would be required to buy huge numbers of printed paperbacks which in some cases were not particularly well produced. The authors would fill their spare rooms with all the copies and spend a great deal of their time desperately trying to sell them all with generally no help from the vanity publisher. Fortunately, choices have evolved. I have taken some of the most popular choices to look at in this book.

Self-publishing

> *"The good news about self-publishing is you get to do everything yourself. The bad news about self-publishing is you get to do everything yourself."*
>
> **Lori Lesko, author**

The ability to self-publish a book without a traditional publisher began around 2009 with Amazon. It started off with a bad reputation as it was difficult for authors to produce good looking books. There was quite a lot of resistance within the industry to accept this new form of publishing and the ability for individual authors to create their own books. It was considered very much a second class way of publishing. However, it opened up the market enormously for individuals with a book idea to publish without the constraints of what traditional publishers were looking for in terms of genre or content. Anything appeared to be possible with this new self-publishing. Ten years on, and self-publishing has become more established and acceptable although I have still come across some incredibly badly formatted and produced books!

What to think about if you are considering self-publishing

- Do you have the expertise to do everything yourself? Proofing, editing and other aspects of publishing are not generally skills that everyone has and often those that have them have worked long and hard to perfect them. The question is, how professional do you want your book to look?

- Is time an issue for you? Have you got the time to learn the new skills you need to publish your book – if you are running a business then your time is going to be limited. You will need to weigh up the value of an hour of your time learning the skills you need against how much you could earn in that same hour if you were working with one of your clients. Chances are it will not be cost-effective. For those with families, it can be difficult enough to put time aside to actually write your book let alone then have to master all the skills to publish it yourself.

- Finding the right people to help you at each stage. This can be quite time-consuming, and scheduling the different skills into your timetable may not be something you want to spend valuable hours organising.

Although this may be thought of as a cheap way to publish, if you are going to do it properly then you are still going to have to pay for specialist services. I am not going to go into this area in too much detail here other than to say that the following chapters will give you information which will help if you decide to take this route.

Assisted/Hybrid publishing

These types of publishers are a halfway house between traditional publishing and self-publishing and that is what Goldcrest Books, my company is. To all intents and purposes a Goldcrest Books' author looks traditionally published and the books we produce are of a high quality. However, particularly in assisted publishing, the authors retain the rights to their books and have the final say on how it looks and where they sell it. The author will take on the financial costs to produce the book. That is generally where the relationship between author and the assisted publisher ends. However some companies, Goldcrest Books included, love to stay in touch with their authors and continue to offer advice and help if needed. At Goldcrest Books we also like to help promote the book throughout our network and when we are at events etc.

All the following steps in this book are part of the service you can expect from a good assisted/ hybrid publisher.

The cost for this type of publishing does vary between publishers and depends also on the length and complexity of the manuscript. However, the cost for producing the book should not necessarily be the prime concern, particularly with non-fiction, as these books can make the author a substantial amount of revenue by upselling their primary business services or products. In addition, non-fiction authors often find that if they have a small quantity of books printed, then being able to sell these directly to their customers can help to recoup the costs of having the book published. These sales do not include a third party, like Amazon, who will take a percentage of the retail price. For example, Goldcrest Books author, Lily Naadu Mensah had 250 copies of her book, *Work your Quirks*, printed via Goldcrest Books. She had a launch event for her contacts and clients who bought the book directly from her. She didn't charge anymore for the book, but received a much better return per copy as she just paid for the printing and delivery. Although her book is available via Amazon, she has since ordered another 500 books and has had events in the UK and abroad where she has signed and sold the copies.

It is possible to buy author copies via Amazon at a reduced price, but traditional printers can generally offer a cheaper price per copy and also give discounts for larger quantities.

How to pick a good assisted/hybrid publisher

There are quite a lot of assisted/hybrid publishers now who can help you publish your book. So how do you pick the right one? Here are a few tips to help you.

- Recommendation or referral is probably the best way to find a publisher – is there anyone in your network who has used one and been happy? It is also useful to know if there are any that have not lived up to expectations so you can be aware if you decide to contact them yourself. I would say that a large proportion of authors enquiring about my company and publishing with us have come via recommendations

- Google search – everyone does this for anything these days. It may turn up a lot of results so looking at the websites of each publisher will give you an idea of the services they offer and also give you a feel for the type of books they are willing to take on

- Can you easily make contact with someone? Are they willing to answer all your questions either in writing or over the phone?
- Does the publisher make it clear whether you retain your rights? Do they have the final say over how your book is produced or where it is sold? If you are not sure what rights to your book are, then we cover this on page 33.
- Do they provide you with a personalised detailed quotation or is it a generic form listing all the services?
- Are you able to pick the services you need or do you have to take the whole publishing package? All the quotations we send out are tailored to the particular enquirer, and generally after a discussion to find out exactly what is needed
- Compare costs as these can vary greatly between companies. It is not always straightforward to compare publishers as each may have slightly different offerings. Some may also add VAT to their prices
- Does the person you speak to or write to sound optimistic about your book? If they don't seem personally interested in it, it

might make it harder to work with them. I do sometimes decide not to take on a book that an author has presented to me if I don't feel that the content of the book is something I would want to publish or tell everyone about

- Will you be dealing with lots of different people during the publishing process or just one? This could be important to you. I am currently working with an author on her second book and I am the only point of contact and deal with all her questions. She told me this is what she really likes as we can get to know each other and we always know exactly what is going on. I like to do this with all my clients so we get to know each other well, which is why some have become good friends and others come back again and again each time they finish writing a new book

- Be very wary of anyone who promises you lots of sales or pressurises you into buying loads of printed copies as part of the deal. How many books you eventually sell will, in the majority of cases, be down to how much work YOU put into marketing your book

- You may have other thoughts about what you want from your publisher, so make a list of your requirements and concerns before you write or speak to each one to make it easier to compare them.

Traditional publishing

This form of publishing is the option that will take the longest amount of time to complete. If you take into account the time you will spend looking for and securing a publisher (or an agent – more about that later) and then negotiating a publishing deal before the actual production process begins, it could be years. An author friend of mine has written a wonderful romantic adventure and did secure an agent fairly quickly. However, about three years on and that agent is still trying to arrange an acceptable publishing deal.

If time is not an issue for you and you want the kudos of being chosen by a traditional publishing house, then at least you will be entering the process with your eyes open. You need to get used to handling the prospect of having your work rejected and to letting someone else make some of the decisions about your book for you.

There is more of a process involved with going this route which I will explain in the coming pages. You can also find information about the top publishers in the UK at the end of this chapter.

Once the publishing house has decided to take on your book you will receive a contract and will need to relinquish the 'rights' (I will explain more about these later) to your book. You may receive a small advance but that depends on the individual publisher and what you have agreed within your contract. More information about contracts is really beyond the scope of this book and you would be advised to seek legal advice before signing. Once a deal has be struck and you have signed your contract, the publisher then decides how your book will look i.e. cover design and interior. You may also be asked to rewrite or change some aspects of your book depending on what the in-house editor wishes. Once the book is published you will receive royalties for each copy sold via your publisher. Publishers tend to promote for short periods when the book is first released, however you will be expected to promote it yourself too. If your book doesn't sell the quantities that the publisher expected then you may be dropped as new authors are taken on. So you need to bear this in mind when you are considering how you wish to publish your book. If traditional publishing is still the way you wish to go then you can contact publishing houses directly or acquire an agent.

Even if you decide to self-publish or use an assisted or hybrid publisher you can still approach a traditional publisher later. My company, Goldcrest Books, published a non-fiction book which the author then decided to take to a traditional publisher. The advantage she had here was that she had a really good looking printed copy and pdf to show the publisher and could also demonstrate that she had been successfully promoting and selling her book too. In this instance, it was Bloomsbury who decided to take the book on and bought the rights from the author. The Goldcrest Books edition was then retired and replaced by the Bloomsbury copy which was given a new cover. I actually found this rather exciting as it showed just what can be achieved if you wish to take your book further.

What is an agent and do I need one?

If you decide to go the traditional route to bring your book to your readers then you have the option to either approach the publishing houses directly or look for an agent. Acquiring an agent is much more common for fiction writers than non-fiction although some agents will deal with both.

A literary agent is the bridge between the author and the traditional publisher. They help publishing houses work through the vast number of manuscripts from authors wishing to be published. Some agencies can receive as many as 200 submissions (manuscripts sent to them) in a week. So doing your homework before submitting your manuscript is vital.

An agent has a huge amount of publishing experience so is well placed to approach specific publishers on your behalf. So you may decide that it would be easier for you to find an agent than to send your work out to numerous publishing houses unsolicited in the hope that one will like your submission enough to publish it. Most publishing houses receive inordinate amounts of manuscripts so will end up with a 'slush pile' which are manuscripts that have not been requested (unsolicited) so it may mean that your work doesn't even get read.

A good agent will probably secure you a better deal with a traditional publisher than you could manage yourself. You won't need to negotiate over any advances or royalty rates. Rights and contracts will be overseen by your agent too. For this service your agent will usually take 15% of advances and royalties, possibly more for translation and overseas sales.

How do I find the right agent for my book?

Researching for the right agent is well worth the effort and will save you time in the long run. Two good resources for finding an appropriate agent in the UK are:

- www.agentsassoc.co.uk
  There is an alphabetical list of members on the website
- The Writers' & Artists' Year book has a comprehensive list of literary agents in the UK and overseas. The listing for each agent

also includes the type of books and genres that they will accept. The book is available via Amazon or from the Writers' and Artists' website at www.writersandartists.co.uk. You can become a subscriber to access listings via the website at www.writersandartists.co.uk/listings

To find an American agent check out the Directory of Literary Agents at www.literaryagencies.com/list-of-literary-agents/

If you find an agent who, from the listing, would theoretically be interested in your book's subject or genre then first visit their website. You may find that there is more than one agent working within the company, each dealing with a particular type or genre of book. Review each individual agent, look at their biographies (most good agent websites will include these). Decide which one you would like to query (submit your manuscript to). It is best not to query more than one agent from the same company at once. Wait to hear back from the one before, if necessary, going on to your next choice. If you wish to submit to agents from different companies then make sure that you let them know who else has received your submission. You will need to carefully study the submissions guidelines on the agent's website. Again check that you can meet the guidelines and that the particular agent is still accepting submissions before submitting your work. If an agent has been swamped with manuscripts then there will be a note on the website saying submissions are closed or not being accepted for the moment. Don't be tempted to submit your manuscript anyway 'just in case' as it will be a waste of your time and the agent will not look favourably on you ignoring guidelines. Much better to try someone else or, if you really like the sound of a particular agent, then check their website in a few weeks to see if the situation has changed and submissions have been opened again.

How do I submit my book to an agent?

Once you have decided on an agent you will need to prepare your manuscript and the other information requested in the submission criteria.

These days most agents prefer to receive information from authors by email, but they will let you know their preferences on the submissions page of their website. Make sure you send exactly what they ask for and no more. Make it as easy as possible for the agents to extract what they need from the information you send them.

Most agents will ask for the following:

- An introductory email to tell them briefly about you and your book, perhaps how you came to write it if there is an interesting story behind it. You could include where you think it would fit into the book market, so genre, categories. Whereabouts would you find your book in a bookshop, for instance? This is probably a question that the agent will be asking herself or himself as she/he looks through what you have sent
- A synopsis of your book. This is an outline of the story or content of your book. The emphasis here is on the word 'outline', an agent doesn't have the time to wade through pages of waffle! Be precise
- The first three chapters of your manuscript – some will ask for this to be pasted into the email rather than sent as an attachment. If you are sending your submission by post then your document should be either 1.5 or double spaced with page numbers on A4 paper. But check the exact submission criteria for each agent

Some other points to remember when sending off your submission are:

- Make sure you are sending the best possible copy of your first three chapters so make sure it is edited and proofed beforehand. As you are only sending off part of the book, you don't necessarily need to have the whole book edited and proofed at this stage. This could save you money initially if you are working to a tight budget
- Put the title of your book and your name into the subject line of the email
- Don't forget to include your full name, a mailing address and phone number to make it easy for the agent to contact you if your work is of interest
- Don't ring the agent to tell them to expect your submission or follow up after you have sent it. It could be some weeks before the agent is able to read what you have sent. If you haven't heard anything after about three months then you could send a polite follow-up unless the agent has already made it clear in the submissions criteria that this is not welcomed
- If you have also submitted your manuscript directly to publishers then make sure you let the agent know which ones

- Don't expect an agent to comment or offer editorial feedback if they are not interested in your book. If this is what you are looking for then you need to get in direct touch with an editor who will expect payment for this type of feedback

Useful contacts for further information and help are:

The Society of Authors (www.societyofauthors.org)

Writers' & Artists' website (www.writersandartists.co.uk/writers/services)

If you decide to contact publishers directly, here are the top traditional publishers in the UK in alphabetical order:

Bloomsbury – the home of Harry Potter.

www.bloomsbury.com/uk/

Hachette – a UK publishing group with 10 publishing divisions.

www.hachette.co.uk

HarperCollins – has published works by Agatha Christie and the Brontë Sisters.

www.harpercollins.co.uk

Pan MacMillan – part of the Macmillan Group – originally published Lewis Carroll, H.G Wells and W.B Yeats.

www.panmacmillan.com

Penguin Random House – once two separate well-known publishers – publishing Roald Dahl's *Matilda*, Margaret Atwood and Danielle Steel.

www.penguinrandomhouse.com

Simon & Schuster – publishing Lynda la Plante and Stephen R. Covey's *The 7 Habits of Highly Effective People.*

www.simonandschuster.co.uk

COPYRIGHT AND OTHER LEGAL MATTERS

This is an area which causes great concern amongst, particularly new, authors. The most common concern is generally relating to copyright. I can give you an overview here of the legal areas that you need to watch out for. If you have any concerns or need more detailed information for your situation then I would always suggest consulting a legal professional.

Copyright

Any material that is considered to be original is eligible for copyright protection and in the UK that also means protection globally. As soon as you put your book idea down on paper or type it on your computer, it is protected by copyright law. This means that your book does not need to be published or 'made available to the public' to be protected. This is a point that often causes confusion.

It is the *expression* of the idea for the book not the idea itself that is protected. This can be illustrated well in the case of Michael Baigent and Richard Leigh, two authors who took on the publishing house, The Random House Group Limited, for breach of copyright in 2006. Baigent and Leigh brought a case against Random House who published Dan Brown's fiction book, *The Da Vinci Code* saying that parts of it were copied from an earlier non-fiction book by them called *The Holy Blood and the Holy Grail.*

The two books explored similar themes, however, the high court ruled that this did not constitute a breach of copyright. The composition and the way their ideas were *expressed* in their book did protect Baigent and Leigh. However, according to Lord Justice Mummery: *'It does not, however, extend to clothing information, facts, ideas, theories and themes with exclusive property rights, so as to enable the claimants to monopolise historical research or knowledge and prevent the legitimate use of historical and biographical material, theories propounded, general arguments deployed, or general hypotheses suggested (whether they are sound or not) or general themes written about'.*[1]

1. www.theguardian.com/uk/2007/mar/28/danbrown.books

Baigent and Leigh lost their case. The two books explored similar ideas but the way they were expressed was fundamentally different.

The author may license his work to give permission for the work to be used under certain conditions while it is under copyright. This licence is provided by the international non-profit making organisation called Creative Commons. Music and photographs as well as blogs and websites can also be covered by Creative Commons licences.

Copyright lasts for as long as the author is alive and for up to seventy years (and sometimes longer in some instances) after the author's death. The exact time can vary between countries. Once the time has elapsed then the author's work can pass into the public domain and can be published or adapted by anyone.

An author doesn't normally pass on the copyright to a publisher.

Plagiarism

This is basically when someone uses the work of another and passes it off as his or her own. The original writer of the work has then had his copyright infringed. It is possible to use part of another author's work but only if permission is sought and granted or it comes under the 'fair use' clause which I mention on the next page.

Use of quotes and lyrics

Generally, if you can get permission from the author of the quote or lyrics it is best, however, you can use small quotes as long as you make it clear who the quote is attributed to.

There is a legal concept of 'fair use' which allows for copyrighted material to be reproduced without permission or paying a fee. This could be if you are reviewing a work and is often used when reporting news and during teaching. If you are giving your opinion or using an author's quote to back up your own writing then it is 'fair use'. If by reproducing this work you are profiting from it financially then it is not considered 'fair use'. However, to be sure that you are not contravening any laws, it is better not to use large amounts of information in this way.

Lyrics are somewhat trickier and it would be best not to reproduce song lyrics in your book unless you can get permission. There is no reason why you shouldn't mention the title and songwriter though.

Using images

It is surprising how many people I meet who still think it is OK to copy any image from Google and use it however they wish. This is not acceptable, and images are subject to copyright just as books are. There are lots of websites online where you can purchase images, www.shutterstock.com, www.dreamstime.com or www.istockphoto.com to mention a few.

If you do purchase an image don't be tempted to buy the smallest and cheapest version. When you come to put it in your book you might find that it is not a high enough resolution and will look blurry. You need 300dpi (dots per inch) for printing unless you are just using it digitally (in your ebook, for example) and then you can use a lower resolution. 150dpi or as low as 96dpi will work.

There are other websites which provide images free of charge as long as the owner of the copyright is cited, and other websites that do not insist on any citation. Do be careful with these though, as there may be many people downloading them and you might find the image you have chosen for your book cover has already been used by someone else. Two examples of websites offering free photos are:

- www.unsplash.com
- www.pixabay.com

Rights

When an author enters into a deal with a traditional publisher all the rights to the author's book transfer to the publisher unless the author has agreed that certain rights can be retained by him/her. There are all sorts of transferable rights that the author can pass on to a publisher or other third parties. I will go through some of those later, but first let's look at the main non-transferable rights.

Moral rights

The moral right of the author does not usually transfer to the publisher. Moral rights didn't enter UK law until 1988 and consist of four rights:

- Paternity – the right to be identified as the author of your work
- Integrity – the right to object to your work being changed or misinterpreted in a way that damages your reputation
- Prevention of false attribution – the right to object to someone pretending to be the author of your work, for example, or someone making changes to your work but still claiming that you are the author of this 'updated' or adapted version
- Privacy – this relates to photos, videos and film

These four moral rights come under the *Copyright, Designs and Patents Act 1988*. These rights must be 'asserted' and an author does this by including a reference on the copyright page of their book. You can see how I have asserted my rights at the beginning of this book.

Transferable rights

Rights that can be transferred are either bought for a flat fee from the author by a publisher, or the purchaser pays an advance and royalties. Transferable rights can include the following:

- Foreign:
  - The right to publish the book in its original language and in a specific country. This will not include the country of origin. So the rights to a book published in the UK could be sold to a publisher in the USA who could then only publish within that country
  - Translation rights. There are separate rights for each language and countries can also be specified here. So a German publisher could buy the rights to publish a book in the German language and just in Germany, or other countries depending on the agreement between the buyer and the seller

- Serial: Selling the rights to a newspaper or magazine
- Audio: These can be full length or abridged versions of the book
- Large print: Usually sold via specialist publishers and mostly for libraries
- Braille: These rights are generally transferred free of charge
- Screen: This covers TV and film rights so if you wanted to see your book made into a film, the rights would be sold to a production company
- Radio dramatisation: Usually handled via the BBC in the UK

There are book fairs all over the world that deal in selling rights so publishers can negotiate terms etc face to face. In the UK the London Book Fair, which takes place once a year usually in March, is where thousands of publishers from all over the world congregate to negotiate rights deals. It can be a lucrative business for both publisher and author.

You don't need to sell all your rights to the publisher of your book. I know authors who have entered into a traditional publishing deal for the printed copy of their book, but have retained the rights to the digital version (ebook). This means that the author could self-publish the ebook or sell those rights to a publisher who specialises in ebooks, for example.

Licensing Agencies

This is particularly interesting to those of you with a non-fiction book. In the UK, the Copyright Licensing Agency (CLA) collects fees from companies, institutions or third parties who wish to use copyrighted material. If you think your book may be copied and used in this way then it may be worth joining the scheme. I remember my father was still receiving a small income years after his technical books were published as they were used within universities. Lecturers would need copies of some pages to use in their courses and my father received a small amount for each copied page.

Libel

If you include a false statement in your book about someone, this could be family, friends or someone you don't actually know, and it has an adverse effect on their life or work, you could be sued for libel. So be sure of your facts because it will be down to you to prove what you have written is true rather than the person affected (plaintiff) to prove those facts are false.

If you are writing fiction and base one of your characters on someone you know, you need to be really careful. Changing the name might not be enough. You must make sure that it is not possible for anyone to guess who the real person behind your character is, and to cover yourself further you must make it clear on the copyright page of your book that any similarity is coincidental, if indeed it is. I know a number of authors who to be doubly sure have had rather odd names for their characters as they didn't want to choose a name that someone might actually in reality have. There is an interesting article by an American lawyer who explains libel in fiction in more detail here:

www.copylaw.com/new_articles/real_people_in_fiction.html

If you have a legal concern you should contact a lawyer. You can find one local to you or you could try the website www.justanswer.co.uk where you ask your question online and receive a response from a lawyer pretty quickly, along with the cost for answering the question. This could be a cheaper option than sitting in a lawyer's office.

HAVE YOU GOT ALL THE PARTS YOU NEED?

So you've written your novel or put together the information for your non-fiction book. But is there anything else you should be considering? Have you got all the parts you need in your book?

There are a number of parts to a book which are either legally required or would enhance your book. Books are generally made up of three distinct sections in which these parts are arranged. The sections are:

- Front matter
- The interior
- Back matter

Each of these sections includes several parts which you might not yet have considered including in your book. So let's have a look at each of these sections and their parts in the next three chapters.

FRONT MATTER

The following list outlines pages you must or can add to the beginning of your book and are known collectively as front matter. I have included them below in the order that they would usually be found. Obviously, you don't need to include all these pages and this is not an exhaustive list but these are the main ones you will come across.

Frontispiece

An illustration on the verso (left side of a book page spread) which faces the recto (right side of a book page spread). I have published a number of books with a frontispiece which has been a map or series of maps. Putting them here makes it easier for the reader to locate them when they are needed as a reference. It also adds interest at the beginning of the book.

Title Page

This page just includes the title and sub-title of the book if it has one. The publisher may also include their logo on the bottom of this page. I usually do this with the books that Goldcrest Books publish. It is also a great page to sign a book for your reader as there is usually plenty of space for a message and your signature. The copyright page is usually found on the back of this page.

Copyright Page

This is an essential part of any book and there are certain phrases that need to be included here for legal reasons. What exactly is written will depend on the content of your book but you do need to include the © symbol, date, publisher details and ISBN (more about the ISBN later). You won't need to worry about creating this page unless you are self-publishing. Goldcrest Books' authors find it a relief that this will be created for them.

Dedication

Sometimes authors like to acknowledge someone really special who has perhaps been the inspiration for the book or who will find the book particularly important. When I published my colouring book, *Colour Me Inspired*, I dedicated it to my aunt as I wanted to find a public way to acknowledge what she means to me. I also knew that she would enjoy the colouring.

Epigraph

This is a short quote or saying which is put at the beginning of the book or before a chapter begins. It can be used to introduce the theme of the chapter to follow and is certainly proving more and more popular in the books that Goldcrest Books is publishing. It can be used in fiction or non-fiction, but should only be used if it adds something to the content that follows.

Table of Contents

I'm sure you know what this is already, but it is important to recognise that this may be one of the first pages that a reader will look at when deciding whether to buy your book. So make sure it is as interesting and relevant to the content as possible. If you are a fiction writer then there is no need to include a table of contents in your printed book, particularly if it is just a list of chapter numbers.

The table of contents could also be followed by a separate list of figures (diagrams, graphs, drawings, tables or photographs) included in the book. If there are a number of tables then these are sometimes grouped together in another list.

Foreword

That is for***eword*** not for***ward*** as I so often see it written. Not generally found in fiction books, this is a short piece which is not written by the author. It explains why readers should read the book. It could be written by an industry professional or someone who has benefited from the book content.

It is generally followed by the name and title of the writer (sometimes location and/or date) and can also include a web address.

Preface

Written by the author telling readers how and why the book came to be written. The author generally signs off at the end of the piece with their name. A preface is generally reserved for academic and technical books although it can work for a memoir.

Introduction

In non-fiction, this could be after the preface or instead of it and introduces the readers to the main topics of the book so they know what is coming next. In fact it is similar to a preface and can also include information about the author which is relevant to why or how the book has been written.

Fiction books don't need a foreword, preface or introduction, but they might need a prologue.

Prologue

This is useful to introduce important background information to a story. It can make the reader aware of some earlier event or situation which helps them to understand the plot of the book. Not all fiction books need a prologue so only include one if it enhances the understanding of the main story.

Reviews

These are becoming more popular in both paperbacks and ebooks. The review page is either on the inside page of the front cover or on a separate page before or after the title page. This page is important when the book will be displayed in bookshops or where readers look before they buy. It is also used in ebooks and works well, particularly on Amazon's 'Look Inside' feature as these advance reviews can be read by potential buyers.

THE INTERIOR

Obviously, you know that this is the section where your chapters will be, but there are a few other parts you may wish to consider adding to this section.

Part Opening Page

Added to divide up a book into logical divisions which will help the reader navigate the book. This can work well with fiction when perhaps there are different time periods or when the separate parts of the book focus on one particular character. It can work just as well with non-fiction. I worked with Paolo Ballardini on his book, *That Moment - Emotions in Travel*, which was divided into eight sections. Each section highlighted a different emotion and the part opening page had the emotion as the title with a short sentence of what that emotion meant to him underneath. It was a great way to leave the one emotion behind and introduce the next.

Chapter Opening Page

This page only has the chapter title on a page and could include a quote, for example. The reader then turns the page to begin reading the next chapter.

If you have a book with lots of chapters then this would be a little excessive. However, it can work well with business books that have just a few main chapters.

Footnotes

Footnotes appear at the bottom of the page and cite references or give additional information which enhances the reader's understanding or interest. They are marked by a small number in the text and are usually a smaller size than the rest of the text on the page. If there is a great deal of footnotes or they are quite lengthy then they can be placed all together at the end of the chapter to which they relate. One of my clients created a book which would have had so many footnotes throughout the book that he chose to include them all in a separate book to accompany the first. This is somewhat unusual though.

Epilogue

Found at the end of the main body or interior of a fiction book. It normally reveals what happens to the characters after the final chapter. It is a way to wrap up loose ends or give the reader additional information about what the characters are doing now their main story is over.

It could also be included if story-telling is used as part of a non-fiction book or memoir.

Not to be confused with an afterword which can be written by someone other than the author and discusses particular topics or aspects of the story.

Conclusion

If you have written a non-fiction book then you will have a conclusion rather than an epilogue. Do you have a clear conclusion to your book? Have you pulled all the information you have given to your reader together so they know what to do next or how to progress after they finish reading your book? This can also be an important part of non-fiction.

BACK MATTER

As the name makes clear, the following parts of a book appear at the back after the main interior part of the book. As with the front matter this is not a completely exhaustive list but contains the main elements you will come across in your writing.

Postscript

An after-thought; hopefully you won't need this! However, it is sometimes used to dramatic effect or to give further information to the reader.

For example:

As a postscript to this chapter, she did finally manage to raise all the money she needed to complete the project.

Or

Postscript: he did end up proposing but it took him five years!

Afterword

This discusses aspects of the story or how the book came to be written. It is not necessarily written by the author.

Appendix

Not to be confused with the little organ in our body that for years we didn't think had any function! In a non-fiction book, an appendix is additional reference material or diagrams to supplement a topic in the book. A book can have more than one appendix in which case the section would be headed up 'Appendices'.

Addendum

This is similar to an appendix except it contains new information that was not available when the book was first published so would typically not be in a first edition or print run of a book.

Chronology

Useful in historic works and is basically a timeline of events in the order in which they occurred.

Glossary

Traditionally included in the back matter, the glossary can also appear at the front of the book. This contains words that may not be immediately understood by the reader or may be in a different language. One of the romantic novelists I work with, Lizzie Lamb, sets most of her books in Scotland and always includes a glossary which also explains how to pronounce the Gaelic words. It is informative and useful but also adds an additional fun element to her books.

Bibliography

List of works cited in the main body of the book. These are generally cited in a particular format and these days include webpages and the date they were accessed.

List of Contributors

This list could also be in the front matter or part of the Acknowledgements section. It is important to recognise all those people who have contributed in some way to the book, for example, with non-fiction perhaps you interviewed them about their particular area of expertise or have asked their opinion on a topic relevant to the content of your book and have included their responses within a chapter. In the back of my colouring book you will find a list of contributors which includes the name and title of each contributor along with a biography and website details. My hope is that readers will look up those contributors and may even find some of their products and services of use. As I valued their contributions to my book, I wanted to find a good way to thank them, and making my readers aware of who they are, what they do and where they can be found was my way of doing that.

Index

This is generally just used in non-fiction. For example, your book spans a great many topics or areas that may be new to the reader or when you want your book to be used as a reference so the reader dips in and out of it. In that instance, an index is useful to help them navigate the more detailed content and quickly direct them to the information they are searching for. This book is rather short for an index and in this case the table of contents can serve to orientate the reader through it.

If you want to include an index in your book you could use Word or another software package to create one, however, I find that a good index is best created by a trained indexer. If you wish to include one with your book then a good place to start would be the Society of Indexers (www.indexers.org.uk/find-an-indexer/directory) or the American Society for Indexing if you are based in the USA (www.asindexing.org).

Colophon

In modern books this can describe all or some of the following details:

Publisher name and location, typeface, the book's designer, illustrator, printing company details and type of paper.

Traditionally this was always at the end of the book, however it can now be found at the front of the book as part of the copyright page.

Acknowledgements

The Acknowledgement page can appear at the front or back of the book and mentions all those people who have helped the author in some way with the book. In the case of a business book, for example, this can include contributors (unless these are listed separately elsewhere), industry professionals, colleagues, family and friends.

Novelists may want to acknowledge someone who has helped with researching a place or a job that one of the characters has in the book. Family members are often included too as they have provided support, encouragement or a steady supply of cups of tea – a jolly important author writing aid!

Acknowledgement can be spelt with or without an 'e' before 'ments'. Without the 'e' is the preferred US English spelling.

About the Author

This is another important page to include and is particularly good if the author can include a photo. Readers these days like to know about the person behind the words in both fiction and non-fiction. Obviously, it is crucial with, for example, a business book as the author wants to be able to promote products and services or a business connected with the content of the book. It is also an important part of business branding. So including contact details and social media links is important too. These details can also be included on a separate page headed up something like 'Contact the author' if you prefer. The important thing is that you make it as easy as possible for the reader to find out more about you and contact you directly if that is what you wish.

EDITING – WHAT SORT DO YOU NEED?

Once your book gets to a publishing company then it will be a commissioning editor who will review your manuscript and decide whether to accept it. They will also study your submission to help with making their decision. However, there are other types of editors who you may need when writing your book.

If you are going the traditional route or through an agent, you need to make sure that the first three chapters you send have been edited and proofed[2] as you want to present the best possible version to prospective agents or publishers. It shows professionalism and commitment to your writing.

When writing fiction it is imperative that you have a good editor check your work to make sure

---

2. See 'How do I submit my book to an agent?' page 23

that you keep your readers attention throughout your story. How well you edit and proof your book can make a difference to the reviews you will achieve for your book. You want to make it as easy as possible for the reader to actually read; the words need to flow off the page and the story needs to be engaging so you do get those 5* reviews.

However, it is important to find an editor who will still allow your voice to shine through your writing and not create something accurate but rather generic. Before an editor decides to take on your work they should ideally request either part or the whole manuscript to review. This means that they can decide whether the content is something they wish to work with and can more accurately quote you for the job. This is certainly the way we work at Goldcrest Books with our authors and is also why I have more than one editor in my team so I can find the one who I think would do the best job for the author's subject matter. But it is still up to the individual editor to decide whether they wish to take the book on or not.

OK, that might sound quite straightforward, but there are a number of different types of edits that you could have on your book. So what are they and what sort do you need?

The main types of book editing are:

- Copy editing
- Line editing
- Developmental editing

So let's look at these in more detail.

Copy editing

This is similar to proofreading in that the copy editor is looking for grammatical, spelling and punctuation errors, but a proofreader will not suggest any large changes to the work. The copy editor is also checking style, language and usage. This may also include suggesting some rewrites.

Line editing

This form of editing focusses on style rather than grammar and spelling. As the name suggests, it involves editing the manuscript line by line so effectively sentence by sentence. A line edit tends to be more to do with how the words are interpreted and is more subjective than a copy edit. It will look at specific word choice and whether there would be a better alternative. It looks at avoiding clichés and tightening up sentences which may mean cutting out superfluous words.

In fiction books, if there is a scene full of suspense and drama but the language doesn't match then a line editor will ensure the tone is changed so it does match the scene.

Developmental editing

The most comprehensive of all the types of editing, a developmental edit will be useful to the author who has written a couple of drafts but is still not sure about basic elements within the book. Examples of this would be the structure or sequence of events, or in fiction it could involve the characterisation or the setting/location of the novel too.

Hopefully now you will have a better idea of the type of editing you need for your book. Not everyone needs one or all of these. If you are a business owner used to writing copy anyway then you might find that all you need is a good proof which we will come onto later.

How do you find an editor?

You can ask your contacts for recommendations or look at the Chartered Institute of Editing and Proofreading at www.ciep.uk. It has a directory of members where you can search for someone to suit your specific book topic or genre. Each member is graded according to their experience, skills and the work that they do. The member profile includes their location, contact details and services offered.

If you are looking for an editor in the USA then try the Society of Editing which has a hire directory at www.aceseditors.org/resources/for-hire

"The beautiful part of writing is that you don't have to get it right the first time, unlike, say a brain surgeon"

Robert Cormier, American author

THE IMPORTANCE OF PROOFING

It is amazing how good our brains are at filling in the gaps when we read something. You know what I mean, sentences with words missing or spelt wrongly – we just don't see it. Have you seen that exercise on the internet which is a series of words with all the letters jumbled up? Yuo cna sitll raed tihs eevn thugoh it is msiselpt. OK, you might say *well why is it so important if I can still read it?* A book full of proofing errors looks unprofessional and reflects badly on you as the writer. It may also result in you getting bad reviews even though the content of your book is good and warrants a great review.

Having someone independent read your work is important as they are more likely to pick up the mistakes because they are reading your work for the first time. If you have read and reread yours it is unlikely that you will be able to spot all the mistakes as you know your writing so well by that stage and know what is coming next.

That is why it is important to have your book professionally proofread as it could be full of errors that you have missed and not just spelling mistakes; there are all those tricky points of grammar which we always say we never learnt at school! Those pesky commas or full stops can change the meaning of a statement so easily. Have you seen the road sign advising: 'Hunters please use caution when hunting pedestrians using walk trails'? Or your choice of words can change the meaning of a sentence. Like the notice in the café warning that: 'Tables are for eating customers only'. See what I mean? These are funny but yours might be embarrassing!

Even though a book has been professionally proofread there is still the chance that something may be missed. I don't think I have read many books that have been absolutely perfect but aiming for as near perfect as possible is a good decision and the odd mistake can be forgiven or may not even be noticed.

Having your book proofread is part of the publishing process unless you decide to self-publish. Then you will need to find a professional proofer. Asking for recommendations from within your network of contacts can be a great place to start, but don't be led down the road of '*my niece read my book, she's good at English*'. Make sure the recommendation is a professional one – you could ask for an example of a book that they have already proofread. You could also look at the Chartered Institute of Editing and Proofreading at www.ciep.uk which I suggested before when looking for an editor.

Proofreading is not the same as the forms of editing that we have looked at in the preceding chapter. An editor will focus on your manuscript as a whole and make sure that it makes sense and that there are no large inconsistencies. For instance, in chapter 3 a character may have long blond hair blowing in the wind but by the time the reader gets to chapter 10 it is short and dark! Or an historical character is using language which would have been inappropriate or non-existent in that era. After your manuscript has been edited and you have taken on board any suggestions made by your editor to improve your writing, and when you are entirely satisfied that you have the best possible version of your book, then that is the time to give it to a proofreader. The proofreading will then ensure that grammar, punctuation and spelling are accurate and consistent. The editor may have supplied you with a stylesheet which will also help the proofreader work on your manuscript. This is generally the last time that the author will be able to make changes to the manuscript before it goes into the production phase of publishing. Goldcrest Books' authors have one more opportunity to check their words after the whole book has been typeset and is ready for printing, but this may not be the case with all publishers. So make sure you make a final thorough check of your work before going any further.

I have given you a lot of information to digest so far and I think you deserve a little light relief. The next two pages will provide just that.

A little light relief...

It was a beautiful sunny day and the sky was cloudless and blue. A woman was swimming in the crystal clear waters of the sea.

Suddenly she saw a big grey fin break the surface of the water.

"Help a shark!" she cried out.

The lifeguard on the shore looked out to sea and jumped down from his vantage point.

"OK," he called back and then turned around and ran up the beach towards the town.

"Hey, where are you going?" shouted the woman.

"I'll be back soon," he called over his shoulder.

Why is he leaving me here to be eaten by this shark? the woman thought to herself.

A few moments later, the lifeguard was seen running back to the sea with a big box in his arms. As he waded into the water he lifted the box and threw the contents in the direction of the woman who was now being circled by the shark. Fish heads, crab claws and sundry other seafood parts splashed into the water around her.

"What are you doing?" the woman screamed.

"You said help a shark so I have some food for it," the lifeguard answered.

"But the shark will eat me!" she shouted back angrily. The lifeguard didn't hear her as he was already on the way back to his vantage point, having completed his mission.

"Hey, narrator," the woman called out. "You have the author's voice. Why is she trying to kill me off, I thought she liked me?" The narrator answered quietly that he thought it wasn't personal, but was just a point of grammar, a missing comma to be precise.

The shark opened its enormous jaws. It was probably the biggest great white shark anyone had ever seen and the woman disappeared down its throat.

Postscript: The author was surprised at the outcome but thought the storyline would be great for a film. The narrator stepped in at this point and said he thought it had already been done... der, der!

TYPESETTING

If you are intending to go the self-publishing route then you will need to format your manuscript yourself so that it is acceptable to sell via Amazon. You have probably used Word or the Mac equivalent to write your manuscript. Remember if you are going to format the interior yourself you will not be working on an A4 page anymore so you will have to change the size of your document to match the size of the book you wish to create.

There are also a number of typesetting terms that you need to think about. I have listed some of them here. To go into detail on this subject is beyond the scope of this book and I could probably write another whole book on how to typeset!

- Hyphenation – this would not normally be used in a book so splitting words across lines or even pages should be avoided

- Widow – this is the last line of a paragraph which appears at the top of the following page on its own. It can be rather distracting for the reader and should be avoided at all costs

- Orphan – this is the same as a widow but appears alone at the bottom of a page. Try and avoid these if at all possible, but the odd one in a book seems to be acceptable these days, particularly if it means that the text on the rest of the page is better spaced

- Runt – this is a single short word at the end of a paragraph which just drops onto the next line. If it is a two-letter word like 'it' for example, this can be distracting and easily missed by the reader and can interrupt the reading flow. It is a good idea to tweak the sentence formatting so that it can remain on the line above if possible

- Consistency of headings and sub-headings – decide on the size and look of headings you are going to use. Format them as styles so that when creating an ebook they can be picked out automatically to form the table of contents

- Use of running headers – these are the titles at the top of each page which generally show either the author name or title of the book along with the chapter heading

If you have chosen to go either the traditional or the assisted/hybrid publishing route, you don't need to worry about typesetting your book interior. I generally send my authors a couple of possible samples for an interior where I think about the size of the book, the typeface (font and size), margins, running headers, and page numbers. Sometimes I will also create a graphic which is added onto the chapter pages. I love this part of the publishing process and enjoy being creative and putting together an interior to suit the content and the cover of the book. My authors, on the other hand, are delighted that they don't have to do this work themselves and are more than happy to leave me to come up with suggestions, and then all they need to do is relax and choose what they want.

WHAT IS AN ARC AND HOW CAN IT HELP PROMOTE YOUR BOOK?

An ARC (Advance Review Copy) is an unfinished copy of your book which has not yet been published. It may be at the editing or proofing stage. An ARC is clearly marked on the front page so readers know that it is an unfinished copy and will probably contain spelling or grammatical errors. An ARC is also sometimes called a galley copy, particularly by publishers. Galley copies often include a front cover although this may not be the final version that is used when the book is published. ARCs can be in the form of a simple PDF or a mock-up of the actual book.

How is an ARC used?

Both self-published authors and publishers can use an ARC to gather feedback.

Obtaining feedback before publication can be really beneficial as it could highlight an area in a business book where the content has been misunderstood by the reader, for instance, or alert the writer to a topic which has not been included in the book or needs to be expanded upon. For fiction, the reader may not identify with a character in the way you had imagined or might offer further insight into a location or event covered in the story. They can even pick up on inconsistencies in the storyline which you, as the writer, have missed.

Another important area where an ARC can be useful is with garnering reviews. Reviews are so important to an author and can help to establish credibility for your book and ultimately help sell more books. I'm sure you look at the reviews section on Amazon before you decide whether to buy a particular book or one of its competitors. If you use the 'Look Inside' feature on Amazon or are in a bookshop you might pick up a book with a page of reviews at the front of it which could also persuade you to buy. But how do you get reviews into your book before it is printed and published? This is where an ARC is used. You can select a small number of trusted contacts to become your beta readers.

What is a beta reader?

A beta reader is not an editor or a proofer, but a layperson who is willing to read your book. The beta reader is given a free ARC and is asked to read it with a view to giving feedback. You can give your beta readers direction if you wish or questions to answer if you are looking for specific feedback, for example, in a fiction work:

- Are there any areas of the storyline which are confusing or is there something missing?
- Does the story flow easily from chapter to chapter? Is the pace of the story working?
- Is the dialogue believable and natural or is it stilted and not fitting with the character?
- Is there a satisfying ending to the book?

These are just a few examples of the sort of feedback you might want to collect from your beta readers for your fiction book. However, beta readers can be used just as well for non-fiction and can comment on the content, structure, and ease of reading, or again you could ask them to answer specific questions. Don't forget they are not professionals so can't be expected to find all your grammatical errors, for example.

However you ask for it, you want constructive feedback that will help you to hone and perfect your writing. You also want to have more than one beta reader – at least three and up to six works well.

Who makes a good beta reader?

Friends and family would probably love to be your beta readers, but do avoid them where you can as they generally will not give you useful feedback. You need to choose someone who will be honest and is not afraid to voice any concerns they have about your book. Here are a few suggestions of where to find beta readers:

- Your connections/email list
- Someone in your target audience – your ideal reader would be a great person to really test the water, so to speak
- Look to any writing groups that you belong to
- Social media – can you ask someone in a Facebook group or one of your followers? You might actually find groups who offer to read each other's work
- Someone within your industry if you are writing a business book
- Use a company that provides beta readers – there will be a cost for this service

- Use a site like NetGalley – more about that later

In addition to giving honest and constructive criticism you also need your beta readers to be reliable. Some people will willingly accept your request but may not have the time to spend on reading your work, so choose wisely. It also helps all your beta readers if you set a deadline by which you need their feedback. You could also simply ask the question 'have you really got time for this?' They are giving their time free of charge but do need to know that it is important to you that you receive their feedback and within the timescale you have set. Don't forget to thank them when you have received their thoughts on your book – a signed copy of the final published version goes down well too.

What is NetGalley?

NetGalley (www.netgalley.co.uk) is a website where authors and publishers can find book reviewers and begin to market their book. There is a fee for this but it is free for reviewers to request digital copies and leave feedback.

You will need to register and then you can list your book for up to six months. There are also a number of marketing packages that you can choose from to help catch the eye of potential reviewers. These vary in price from about £65 to over £1,000.

Endorsements

Another good use of an ARC is to seek endorsements for your book. These can be printed on the cover of the book and are an excellent way to help market your book, particularly if it is endorsed by a celebrity, industry influencer or well-known author.

Endorsements are different from reviews as they are usually short sentences showing support or approval for the book rather than feedback. One of my authors, Enton Barefoot, was lucky enough to receive two endorsements for his book *Laid Bare*, both from 'A' list celebrities. We used these on the front and back covers of his book and on the Amazon description webpage.

Endorsements are a great addition to a cover as the potential reader is assured of the book's quality and that it is a credible source of information.

Whether you are soliciting reviews or endorsements, make sure you leave plenty of time for the recipients of your ARC to respond to your request.

COVER DESIGN – DOS AND DON'TS

The saying goes that you shouldn't judge a book by its cover but that is exactly what we all do, isn't it! You probably scroll down the list of books on Amazon and stop at those that are the most eye-catching. So your book cover needs to be right.

The best way to create the most suitable and appealing cover is to use a book designer or someone who really knows what they are doing. The look of your cover can have an impact on sales, and I know authors who have changed their covers when sales began to wane to find that they started to sell more after the new cover was released.

Here are a few dos and don'ts for you to consider.

- Do make sure you have confirmed your book title first – you need a design that matches the title as well as the content

- Do think about your audience when you are thinking about your cover
- Do use Amazon to check for other covers in your book's genre or subject matter. You can then decide if you want to align your cover with those or strike out on your own. The latter is perhaps more risky as the reader may not know exactly what to expect from your book, but on the plus side it will make you stand out from the crowd
- Don't use templates – you want your cover to be unique
- Do keep it simple – less is definitely more
- Do make sure to use good high resolution images and...
- Don't stretch them to fit the cover as they could become blurry
- Do pay attention to fonts and make sure to choose ones that are easy to read
- Don't make fonts too small – reduce the number of words rather than the font size
- Don't use too many different fonts on a cover – again, less is more
- Do avoid clichés

- Don't use too many colours as it can make the cover difficult to interpret or text difficult to read. A professional will use their intuition as a designer or a colour wheel to make sure that the chosen colours will balance with each other
- Do reduce your finished cover to a thumbnail – is the title still legible, does it still look appealing/eye-catching? This is important to check as it will show on Amazon as a thumbnail when potential readers are scrolling through pages

If you are using a publisher for your book then all these points will be taken into consideration when your cover is created for you. Depending on which publishing route you take will determine how much input you have on your final cover. With my authors some have an idea of what they want so we work on that first. Others do not know what they want at all which is also OK. We create a draft or two and work from there so between the author, me and the designer we come up with a cover that the author loves.

It is also important to find a designer that matches your type of book. Goldcrest Books has a number of designers to choose from, all with different strengths. I make the choice on who would be best suited depending on whether the book is non-fiction or fiction, the genre of the book and any thoughts that the author already has about the type of cover they want.

As I have already mentioned, a good place to start when thinking about your cover is Amazon. Look for books in the same genre as yours and see what sort of covers stand out to you. Are there any particular trends? Do they all have the same sort of feel? Which do you like and why? Also consider those that you don't like and why. The answers to all these questions will help the designer to create a cover you will love.

WHAT IS AN ISBN?

An ISBN is the number you see with a barcode on the back of a book. The letters ISBN stand for International Standard Book Number and there are agencies all over the world that hold these numbers and to which you can apply to buy one for your book.

A numbering system for books was first introduced in the 1960s to help publishers conduct their businesses more efficiently. It wasn't until the early 70s that one standard numbering system was adopted and that became the ISBN. Up until 2005 all ISBNs consisted of only 10 digits, but this has now increased to 13 probably because of the sheer volume of books being published each year.

If you are self-publishing then you will have to buy your own ISBNs. Traditionally published or authors who have used an assisted/hybrid publisher will have an ISBN assigned to their book and will not need to worry about purchasing their own. In that case, the ISBN will be the property of the publisher and details of that publisher will be included along with the ISBN on the copyright page of the book.

What do the numbers mean?

When you come to buy your ISBN it will be made up of 13 digits. These are divided up into five groups of numbers with hyphens between them. Each group of numbers has a meaning and gives information about the publisher and the title. Each ISBN is prefixed with three digits, generally, 978. These are followed by the country identifier which is the country where the book will be published and where you will have bought your ISBN. The next set of digits identifies the publisher and the following set represents the book title. The final digit is a verification number for the whole of the ISBN.

On the following pages are questions that I am most commonly asked when it comes to ISBNs.

Where on my book do I put the ISBN?

The ISBN is put into the copyright page of every book and is also displayed on the back cover usually as part of a barcode, which are the striped lines you often see along with the number. Retailers can scan the barcode and it gives them information about the title.

Most books include the ISBN and barcode at the bottom of the back cover, generally in the centre or the right-hand side. If you are self-publishing with Amazon, for example, the barcode will always appear in the bottom right corner so bear that in mind when you are thinking about what to put on your cover. You don't want to have important information obscured by the barcode.

Where do I get an ISBN?

If you want to buy your own ISBN, you will need to use one of the licence agencies to acquire your numbers. You can buy them individually or in blocks.

Each country or area in the world has its own agency and you should apply to the agency in the country where you wish to publish your book. So if you are in the UK you will approach the UK agency which is Nielsen (www.nielsenisbnstore.com). If you are in the USA you will be looking at

Bowker (www.bowker.com/products/ISBN-US.html) for your ISBN.

For ISBN agencies in other countries, you can use the following link:

www.isbn-international.org/agencies

How many ISBNs do I need to buy?

Each edition of your book will need a separate ISBN so if you have a paperback, a hardback edition and an audio book then you will need three. You will also need a separate ISBN for your ebook. If you are publishing your ebook to Apple iBooks as well as to Amazon Kindle then you will need different types of files and each of these files will require a unique ISBN. If you have a series then each book in the series will need to have its own ISBN. You may have published your book in English, but want to offer a German or French edition perhaps. Each language will need its own ISBN.

What happens to my ISBN if I update my book?

If you make changes to your book then you will need to change the ISBN too. This doesn't mean that if you find typos in your book and correct them that you need a new ISBN, but if you added an extra chapter or significantly changed the information within the pages then you would need to publish with a different ISBN and it would be a new edition. Changing the cover of your book doesn't necessarily mean you need to have a different ISBN unless for marketing purposes it makes more sense to do so.

Can I change or cancel my ISBN?

Once an ISBN number has been assigned to a book it stays with that book forever and cannot be reused, even if the original book goes out of print. Once assigned, it is not possible to cancel an ISBN if you change your mind and decide not to publish.

When should I buy my ISBNs?

You can buy your ISBNs at any time. You don't need to have published a book to acquire one or even to register it. If you know the title of your book it is a good idea to register the ISBN even if it is not yet in print because it gives the system behind the ISBNs time to distribute that number and make it known to retailers etc.

Do ISBNs have an expiry date?

There is no time limit by which you need to have assigned the ISBN. Once you have bought them they are yours forever, to use as and when you need them.

When do I not need to assign an ISBN to my book?

If you're not going to sell your book you don't need to give it an ISBN. If you are printing it just for friends and family you do not need an ISBN.

If you are just going to self-publish with Amazon, for example, then you don't need to buy your own ISBN as you could choose to use one of the free Amazon numbers. However, it is better and more professional to have your own registered ISBN or that of a publisher as it will make your book available to a wider audience through a variety of retailers all over the world.

Do I need to have my books printed in the same country as my ISBN?

If you have an ISBN from, say, a UK agency, that doesn't mean you must have the book printed in the UK. You can print the book wherever you like but the ISBN must be from the country where you are publishing.

WHICH FORMAT TO CHOOSE FOR YOUR BOOK

There are a number of formats you can choose for your book these days.

- Paperback
- Hardback
- 'Coffee table' type hardback
- Large print – these are generally also hardback books and often used in libraries
- Ebook
- Audio book
- Serialisation in magazines like *Woman's Weekly*
- Picture books – generally for children

I always suggest having at least a paperback and an ebook. However, audio books are becoming much more popular and the choice of genres and non-fiction has grown enormously over the past few years. Although having an audio book as well as a paperback and an ebook will increase the overall costs of publishing, if you are not using a traditional publisher, it is still seriously worth considering this option. People can easily download it to their phones and listen when they are out and about which is sometimes the only available 'reading' time they have.

It is often useful to decide which forms you want your book to take before it is produced, as it might influence how you display the content, whether you use a black and white or colour interior for example. The size you choose for your book may be important to you too. As will the price. Obviously 'coffee table' type books are usually in colour and will be much more expensive to produce, so is the content of your book valuable enough or do the images look professional enough to justify the higher purchase price for your book?

If you want to have a paperback and a large print book then these formats will both include separate typesetting even if the actual size of the book remains the same. This adds to preparation and production costs as the large print will obviously mean that your book contains more pages. If you are funding the book yourself this may influence your decision as to which formats you choose.

Audio books can be narrated by you or you can choose from a range of professional narrators. Which route you choose will also have an impact on production price. However, you should not compromise on sound quality as this will be the difference between your book being read in its entirety or being abandoned early on because the listener didn't like the other noises in the background or your monotone voice, for example.

As there is generally a standard purchase price range for each format of book, it is important to consider costs upfront. If you have a hardback book prepared, for example, and then find that by the time you deduct the print costs per copy there isn't anything left after, say, Amazon, has taken its cut for distribution, it will have been a waste. You may have been better off sticking with just a paperback, for example.

There are standard printing sizes for paperbacks and hardbacks if you are considering a book printer. These may differ slightly from the offerings that Amazon's print on demand service will use so it is also important to decide how you wish to sell the bulk of your books. It may be better to use an Amazon standard size which can then be used by your independent book printer too. You can find a list of the Amazon book sizes here:

https://kdp.amazon.com/en_US/help/topic/G201834180

Considering the variety of formats you wish to choose may also affect the cover design of your book. A portrait aspect is going to look quite different to a landscape aspect cover and then of course audio books are square. This may involve more than one design being produced and will mean that the costs of this would need to be considered too.

And don't forget you can always add more formats to your book choices whenever you want. Your readers may even let you know that they would love an audio book, for example, so you can always add that later when your budget allows.

"When a book leaves its author's desk it changes. Even before anyone has read it, before eyes other than its creator's have looked upon a single phrase, it is irretrievably altered. It has become **a book that can be read**, *that no longer belongs to its maker. It has acquired, in a sense, free will. It will make its journey through the world and there is no longer anything the author can do about it. Even he, as he looks at its sentences, reads them differently now that they can be read by others. They look like different sentences. The book has gone out into the world and the world has remade it."*

Salman Rushdie, ***Joseph Anton: A Memoir***

THE NEXT STEP

We are now pretty much at the end of this book which has taken you through each stage of the publishing process and has given you an overview of those stages and perhaps also quite a lot to think about.

I hope this book has helped you decide what you want to do with your manuscript and has inspired you to take that next step to becoming a published author. After all, by the time you get to the publishing stage, you will have invested hours of your time thinking about, researching and writing your book. So you deserve to see your words in print, don't you think?

Whichever way you decide to publish, the whole process should be fun and exciting. As soon as your book appears on Amazon or you hold that first copy in your hand you will forever be known as a published author! And that really is something to get excited about.

Here are some other steps you can take...

If you are just starting on your writing journey then sign up for my newsletter and receive a copy of *The 4Ps Principle to start writing your first book*. You can download the pdf here:

www.goldcrestbooks.com/download-the-4p-principle-free-guide/

For non-fiction writers:

A book development session could help you with writing your business book at whatever stage you have reached. You can find out more about that here:

www.goldcrestbooks.com/book-development-session/

If you are a business owner, coach or speaker and have a manuscript that is pretty much complete then first off, congratulations! To find out how Goldcrest Books can help you publish, check out this web page:

www.goldcrestbooks.com/publishing/publishing-for-business-experts-coaches-and-speakers/

For fiction writers:

Is your story complete? Check out the web page for fiction writers to see how Goldcrest Books can help you publish:

www.goldcrestbooks.com/publishing/publishing-for-fiction-writers/

For readers:

There is also a web page with some of the books Goldcrest Books has already published (www.goldcrestbooks.com/books). There is quite a variety! You may find some that you would like to read, in which case most are available on Amazon or direct from the author.

"I don't believe in personal immortality; the only way I expect to have some version of such a thing is through my books."

Isaac Asimov
Sci-fi Author

RESOURCES

To make it easier for you to find the resources mentioned in this book, I have gathered them all together for you here.

Finding an agent

For the UK:

www.agentsassoc.co.uk

www.writersandartists.co.uk/listings

For the USA:

www.literaryagencies.com/list-of-literary-agents

Further information:

www.societyofauthors.org

www.writersandartists.co.uk/writers/services

Top traditional publishers in the UK in alphabetical order

www.bloomsbury.com/uk

www.hachette.co.uk

www.harpercollins.co.uk

www.panmacmillan.com

www.penguinrandomhouse.com

www.simonandschuster.co.uk

Using images

To buy:

www.shutterstock.com

www.dreamstime.com

www.istockphoto.com

Free images:

www.unsplash.com

www.pixabay.com

Licensing Agency

Copyright Licensing Agency: www.cla.co.uk

Libel in fiction

www.copylaw.com/new_articles/real_people_in_fiction.html

Finding answers to legal questions

www.justanswer.co.uk

Finding an editor or a proofreader

For the UK:

www.ciep.uk

For the USA:

www.aceseditors.org/resources/for-hire

Finding an indexer

For the UK:

www.indexers.org.uk/find-an-indexer/directory

For the USA:

www.asindexing.org

Finding reviewers

www.netgalley.co.uk

ISBNs

For the UK:

https://www.nielsenisbnstore.com

For the USA:

http://www.bowker.com/products/ISBN-US.html

For other countries:

www.isbn-international.org/agencies

Amazon book sizes

https://kdp.amazon.com/en_US/help/topic/G201834180

ABOUT THE AUTHOR

Sarah Houldcroft has been working with authors for many years. She has a background in sales and marketing as well as publishing, is tech-savvy, and as an avid reader brings a new perspective to the publishing process.

Her writing sessions, workshops and publishing programmes have been very well received and she is often asked to speak at events, writers' days, webinars and Facebook Lives.

Sarah is also the author of *Colour Me Inspired*, a colouring book full of inspirational quotes which is available at www.goldcrestbooks.com/cmi

She lives in Leicestershire in the UK with her son, three mostly disabled dogs and, of course, hundreds of books.

ABOUT GOLDCREST BOOKS

Goldcrest Books International Ltd is a team of publishing professionals, headed up by Sarah Houldcroft, who take great pleasure in the personal touch they offer their clients. They like to think they are as passionate about your book as you are and want to offer the best possible service regardless of where you are in the writing and publishing process.

Being a Goldcrest Books author takes the stress out of publishing your book whether you are a new author or one with several books to your name. Goldcrest Books helps you to be empowered by your writing and publishing journey, not stressed and fearful about the process or technicalities.

See what some of Goldcrest Books' authors think:

"As a business coach and sales trainer, I was busy with my clients but I wanted to finally finish writing my first book called Make Your Mondays Matter. *I was so relieved when I met Sarah who said she could publish the book for me and take away all those headaches of self-publishing. Phew, what a relief! I was thrilled she could do this for me as that was the main thing stopping me. With her skills, passion and patience we have created something I'm very proud of as Sarah brought my ideas for my book to life.*

Sarah and her team advised and formatted my book ready to print and publish. Sarah worked her magic to make it available on Amazon and created my ebook version for Kindle. Saving me so much time. And I'm thrilled to say within the first 3 months after it was first published, Make Your Mondays Matter *won an award and I'm honoured to be a Finalist in the International Book Awards 2019 for Business: Sales Category.*

If you're looking to see your book in print, get in touch with Sarah and you can make it happen. A top team to work with. Thank you, Sarah. Now, I'm off to plan the next one!"

Jo James
Business Coach and Sales Trainer.
Author of the award-winning business book
Make Your Mondays Matter

"As a publishing consultant, Sarah is knowledgeable and competent in the book-writing business! I came to Sarah as a complete novice in this field and she guided and nurtured my writing and publishing ambitions with professionalism and calmness. My book, Work Your Quirks, *would not have seen the light of day without Goldcrest Books and of course Sarah at the helm. If you are looking for someone who has the patience of a saint, yet a strong will to coach you to focus on getting your book published, Sarah is the go-to person. She's a #bookduola in my view — no contest."*

Lily Naadu Mensah
Multi award-winning Coach, Speaker, LinkedIn Makeover Analyst, Author of Personal Branding book, *Work Your Quirks*

"Sarah did an absolutely brilliant job bringing my manuscript to life. She is very knowledgeable about everything publishing related and has a great creative talent for designing inspiring cover artwork and stand-out internal formatting.

I wholeheartedly recommend working with Sarah, who took the stress out of the technical side of publishing a book and managed the whole process, leaving me to focus on the bit I do best – the writing!"

Sarah Kerrigan
Author of *The Travel Secret*

"I have known Sarah Houldcroft since Goldcrest Books published my debut fiction novel, The Caterpillar Girl, *in 2016. Sarah's expertise was invaluable every step of the way, from her editing and proofreading contacts, through to the formatting, printing and eventual publication of the book. It is great to see an independent publishing company thriving, and Sarah deserves every success. I would highly recommend Goldcrest Books' services."*

Adam Longden
Author of *The Caterpillar Girl*
and its sequel *Seaside Skeletons*

CONTACT THE AUTHOR

You can get in touch with me in these ways. I'd love to hear from you.

Website:	www.goldcrestbooks.com
Email	publish@goldcrestbooks.com
Facebook:	Goldcrest Books
	Sarah Houldcroft
Instagram:	Goldcrest Books
LinkedIn:	Sarah Houldcroft
Twitter:	@SarahH_GB

NOTES

Printed in Great Britain
by Amazon

44455795R00064